Never Forget Eleanor

story by **Jason June**   pictures by **Loren Long**

HARPER
An Imprint of HarperCollinsPublishers

To Laura, who never forgets.
—Jason June

To my father, who will never be forgotten.
—Loren Long

Elijah loved doing crossword puzzles with his grandma Eleanor. She always seemed to know every word in the dictionary. As Elijah read the clues, his grandmother sang the answers like they were waiting on the tip of her trunk.

"Seven-letter word for g-ul-ping down," Elijah sounded out.

"*Swizzle!*" his grandmother said. "As in, 'Let's swizzle some lemonade, shall we?'"

"Eight-letter word to show dra-ma-ti-ca-lie?" Elijah sometimes stumbled, but Grandma Eleanor was always there to help.

"So close! Dramatically," she supplied. "L-y sounds like lee. And the answer is *flourish*!"

Grandma Eleanor used her way with words to tell the most beautiful stories about family, friends, and fairy tales. As she spoke, Elijah felt like his grandmother's words danced in the air and wrapped him up in a warm hug.

Legend says

it's good luck when a butterfly lands on your nose.

He never missed Saturday story sessions, where she told tales to the town. There was one story in particular that was both Elijah's and his grandma's favorite.

"It was the stormiest weather in over twenty years the day you were born," Grandma Eleanor would say, looking right at Elijah. "But the sun came out with a flourish as soon as you entered the world."

Grandma Eleanor also remembered faces. Of grocery
clerks, librarians, and folks she met long ago. Elijah loved
when she introduced him to new friends.

Grandma Eleanor never forgot a face,
because each one told a unique story.

Everyone in town called her "Never Forget Eleanor" because there was no word, tale, or friend she couldn't remember.

Until one day . . . there was.

It started small at first.

"Four-letter word for th-ough-t," Elijah read aloud.

Grandma Eleanor paused. "I have no idea. . . . Oh, wait! That must be it: *idea.*"

Then it got bigger.

"It was the stormiest . . . What was it again?"

"The stormiest weather, Grandma," Elijah helped. "Remember?"

Others noticed too.

"All my favorites right here in my yard. What brings you by?"

Elijah was concerned. "It's time for Saturday stories, Grandma. Remember?"

The worried looks on his parents' faces confirmed what Elijah felt in his heart.

Grandma Eleanor was forgetting.

The next week, Elijah, his family, and friendly neighbors gathered for another Saturday story session, hoping she wouldn't forget.

But Grandma Eleanor wasn't in her porch swing.

Elijah searched her house,

"Grandma?"

their favorite café,

café

"Grandma Eleanor?"

and the park.

"Grandma

Nobody could find her. Elijah's head was a jumble of worry. Where could she be? What if she never found her way home? How could he get her back?

Eleanoooooooor?"

Elijah took a deep breath to calm his swirling nerves.

That's when he had an idea—a four-letter word for thought.

Grandma Eleanor loved words.

She adored turning those words into stories.

And she cherished sharing those stories with friends.

Elijah realized his grandmother had shown him what to do all along. Even if she didn't know it.

Elijah painted. Then wrote. And their favorite story came to life.

Elijah placed his signs all over town.

At each word, he asked familiar, friendly faces
to wait and guide his grandmother home.

The trail went past their favorite café,   through the park,

and by the barber shop,

ending . . .

Right on Grandma Eleanor's front porch.
"I forgot how to get back," she said. "But
I saw your story, and I started to remember."

From that day on, when she went to the café through the park and needed to find her way home, Grandma Eleanor followed Elijah's signs.

Sun

Some days, she didn't need them. Other days, she did. But Elijah's words and pictures helped her remember for as long as she could.

Then, like all stories, Grandma Eleanor's eventually came to an end. It was time for Elijah's signs to be put away and for the town to say goodbye.

Elijah knew that even though his grandma was gone, he could help everyone remember her.
He spoke her favorite words.
"We always loved to *swizzle* lemonade and use our pencils with a *flourish!*"

He told her favorite stories.
"It was the stormiest day in over
twenty years. . . ."
And he thanked so many familiar
faces for remembering her with him.